This
Buttons Family
book belongs to

_Li_bary_

_H_W_

Cherry and Charlie and Baby Lou,

We're the Buttons, we're just like you!

And every day there's something new

For Cherry and Charlie and Baby Lou!

First published 2012 by Walker Books Ltd
87 Vauxhall Walk, London SE11 5HJ

10 9 8 7 6 5 4 3 2 1

Text © 2012 Vivian French
Illustrations © 2012 Sue Heap

The right of Vivian French and Sue Heap to be identified as
author and illustrator respectively of this work has been
asserted by them in accordance with the Copyright, Designs
and Patents Act 1988

This book has been typeset in HVD Bodedo

Printed in China

British Library Cataloguing in
Publication Data: a catalogue record
for this book is available from
the British Library

ISBN 978-1-4063-2860-8

www.walker.co.uk

The Buttons Family
Staying with Gran

Vivian French

illustrated by
Sue Heap

WALKER BOOKS
AND SUBSIDIARIES
LONDON · BOSTON · SYDNEY · AUCKLAND

"Guess what?"
Mum said.
"You're
going
to spend
the night
with Gran!"

"But I like sleeping
in MY bed," said Cherry.
Charlie frowned.
"Do we HAVE to?"

"Let's make a list of things Gran needs to know," said Mum. "Like I **HATE** hot milk?" Cherry asked. "And Baby Lou always goes to bed with Teddy?" said Charlie.

"Exactly,"
said Mum.

"And you can tell
me what to pack."

"Toothbrushes!"

"Socks!"

"Pants!"

"Pyjamas!"

"Teddy!"

"Porridge!"
said Charlie.

"Porridge?" Mum stared at him.
"I like porridge," Charlie said.
"Don't you want one of Gran's surprise breakfasts?" Mum asked.
"No," said Charlie, "I only like porridge."

"I'm not sure
I want to go to
Gran's," Charlie
said as they
drove off.
"Don't worry,"
Mum told him.
"I've got the list.
Let's sing
a song!"

"Sing!" shouted Baby Lou,
and they sang all the way.

"Hello!"
said Gran.
"Now, who likes making cupcakes?"
"Me!" shouted everyone.

Cherry and Charlie stirred
cake mix, and Baby Lou helped.
"Are you going now, Mum?"
Charlie asked.
"Yes," Mum said. "Give me
a kiss and I'll see you all in
the morning."

While the cupcakes were cooking they did the washing up.

"Let's have a picnic in the sitting room!" said Gran.

After their picnic they iced the cupcakes.

"One each, and then it's bedtime," Gran said. Charlie yawned. "But I'm not tired."

"Good!" Gran smiled. "You can help me blow up the spare bed before your bath."

They all helped, even Baby Lou.

"Where's Teddy?" asked Baby Lou.
"Oh dear," said Gran, "I haven't
seen Teddy anywhere..."
Baby Lou
began
to cry.

"I know!" Gran said. "This is Horace. He looked after your mum and now he can look after you."

"Your mum liked two kisses," Gran said. "One for goodnight and one for luck." "Silly Mum," said Charlie, but he and Cherry had two kisses each.

"Night night,"
Gran said.

"Night, Gran,"
said Charlie.
"It's nice
here."

Cherry woke up first. "Wake up! We're at Gran's house!"

Gran came
in waving
Mum's list.
"Porridge,
Charlie?"
"Can we have
a surprise?"
Charlie asked.
"Of course,"
said Gran.

Gran's surprise breakfast
was wonderful.

"YUM!" said Baby Lou.

"Would you like a cupcake now you've finished?" Gran asked. Charlie beamed. "Cupcakes for breakfast? **SUPER** cool!"

TOOT! TOOT!
"It's Mum and Dad!"
Charlie shouted.

"You forgot Teddy, Lou,"
said Mum. "Did
you miss him?"
Baby Lou
held up
Horace,
and Mum
laughed.
"Ready to go?"
Cherry and Charlie
looked at each other.

"Do we HAVE to?"

There are six **Buttons Family** books to collect.
Which ones have you read?

New Shoes

Charlie's shoes are too tight!
He says he doesn't want
new ones, but what do
his toes say?

ISBN 978-1-4063-2855-4

Going to
the Doctor

Cherry's got a nasty cold.
How will Mum persuade
her to go to the doctor?

ISBN 978-1-4063-2857-8

Staying with Gran

Cherry, Charlie and Baby Lou have
never stayed with Gran on their
own before. Will Gran make sure
they feel at home?

ISBN 978-1-4063-2860-8

First Day
at Playschool

It's Cherry's first day
at playschool and she's
feeling a little shy.
How will she settle in?

ISBN 978-1-4063-2856-1

The
Babysitter

Mum and Dad are going out.
What do Cherry, Charlie
and Baby Lou think of the
new babysitter?

ISBN 978-1-4063-2858-5

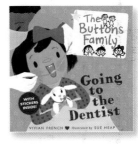

Going to
the Dentist

It's time for the Buttons
to go to the dentist!
How will they get on at
their check-up?

ISBN 978-1-4063-2859-2

Available from all good booksellers